Hello!

can we...
Fix
it?

Written and edited by Brenda Apsley
Stories adapted from original scripts by Jimmy Hibbert, Diane Redmond
and Chris Trengove
Designed by Sally Metcalfe

Based upon the television series **Bob the Builder** © HIT Entertainment PLC
and Keith Chapman, 1998
With thanks to HOT Animation
Text and illustrations © HIT Entertainment PLC, 1999
All rights reserved.

Published in Great Britain in 1999 by
Egmont World Limited,
Deanway Technology Centre,
Wilmslow Road, Handforth,
Cheshire SK9 3FB

Printed in Italy
ISBN 0 7498 4406 X

Bob the Builder™

Contents

It was Christmas Eve, and Scoop, Muck and the other machines in the yard were excited. Dizzy was running around in circles!

Bob came out of his house with a big box. "It's time to decorate the yard for Christmas," he said.

"Brilliant!" said the machines. "Wow!"

Wendy and Scoop came into the yard with a Christmas tree.

"It's the biggest they had," said Wendy.

"And it weighs a ton," said Scoop. "Phew!"

Bob and Wendy decorated the tree.

"You know what I wish?" said Dizzy.

"Erm, no, I give up. What do you wish?" said Muck.

"I wish it would snow!" said Dizzy.

"Oh yeah, me too!" said Roley.

Bob smiled. "There's not much chance of that," he said. "It never seems to snow here at Christmas."

The phone rang and Wendy went to answer it. "It's Mrs Percival at the school, Bob," she said. "She says could you come over at half past four."

"Oh, I forgot!" said Bob. "I said I'd be Father Christmas at the school."

"But why can't Father Christmas go himself?" asked Lofty.

"Well ... er ... he's very busy," said Bob. "He needs people like me to help him."

Scoop could not believe it. "You mean you're one of his helpers, Bob?" he said.

Bob smiled. "You could say that," he said.

"Bob is one of Santa's helpers," said Scoop. "Wow!"

Just then something small and white and cold fell out of the sky. It landed on Dizzy. It was a snowflake. "Look, it's snowing!" she said. "Brilliant."

"Yippee!" said Scoop. "Your wish has come true, Dizzy. We're going to have a white Christmas."

The roof was soon covered in a soft layer of snow. It was good fun.

"Wheee!" said Dizzy, turning round and round.

Muck and Scoop had a snow fight. Muck threw snow at Scoop. Scoop threw snow at Muck. Even Lofty threw some. Well, a little tiny bit ...

Wendy came out with a cup of tea for Bob.

"Oh, thanks, I – whooblfff," said Bob as a big blob of snow hit him and dropped into his tea.

"Whoops! Sorry, Bob," said Muck.

"No harm done," said Bob. "Except that my tea's cold now."

"I know," said Wendy. "Why don't you stop snow fighting and build a snowman?"

"Yeah, great idea Wendy," said Scoop.

The machines were showing Bob their snowman when Wendy came out of the office. "Farmer Pickles is snowed in, Bob," she said. "He needs you and Scoop to dig him out urgently."

When Bob had fitted Scoop with his snow plough, they were ready.

"Can we dig it?" said Bob.

"Yes we can!" said Scoop and the others.

"Er, yes, I suppose so," said Lofty.

Just after Bob had gone, Wendy found his phone. "Bob's forgotten his mobile phone," said Wendy. "Will you take it to him?" she asked Dizzy.

Dizzy set off. It was snowing hard, and she was soon covered in snow. It made her shiver and shake. "Brrr," she said. "It's cold. I'll take a short cut across the field."

Spud the scarecrow had made an ice slide. "Wheeee!" he said, and slid right off the end! He rolled and rolled across the field.

"Stupid ice slide," he said, then stopped. There was a big mound of snow in front of him. It was wobbling and shaking.

"Oh, no!" said Spud. "A snow monster. Heeeeelp!"

Spud ran all the way to the farm house, where Scoop was clearing away the last of the snow. "Heeelp!" said Spud. "It's a s...s...snow monster!"

"I've never seen one of those," said Bob. "Let's go and have a look at it."

The snow monster was still in the field. "Er, hello," said Bob.

"Is that you, Bob?" said the monster.

"It knows you!" said Scoop.

"Course I know him, it's me, Dizzy!"

"What are you doing here, Dizzy?" Bob asked.

Dizzy shivered. "I was bringing your mobile phone. I took a short cut and got stuck. I'm f...f...freezing!"

"We'd better get you home then," said Bob. "Come on."

Dizzy was soon back at the yard.

It was time for Bob to go to the school.

Wendy had made Muck look like a sleigh, Dizzy was dressed as a reindeer and Bob came out of the house in his Father Christmas outfit. "Muck, Dizzy you look brilliant," said Bob.

"And so do you, Bob," said Wendy.

"Ho, ho, ho!" Bob said in his best Father Christmas voice. "Happy Christmas!"

The children at the school had a lovely time, and so did Bob, Muck and Dizzy. It was late when they got home, and they were soon fast asleep.

The next morning, Bird whistled to wake up Roley.

"It's Christmas!" said Roley. "Happy Christmas, Bird."

Dizzy found a present. "He's been!" she said. "Father Christmas has been. Yippee!"

Bob came out of his house. "You lot are up early," he said.

"Yeah, it's Christmas," said Scoop, "Happy Christmas, Bob."

Wendy arrived at the yard carrying presents. "Happy Christmas, everyone."

"Look Wendy, Father Christmas has left presents," said Muck.

Bob smiled. "And he didn't need any help from me this time," he said. "Happy Christmas!"

Don't forget your phone, Bob!

Wendy

All About BOB

Bob is a builder. He lives in a house in his building yard with his cat, Pilchard. Bob can build, fix and mend just about anything.

Bob's team of machines live in the yard too. Bob just can't understand computers! He has a mobile phone, but he often forgets to take it to jobs and to switch it on! Then, if it does ring, he can't find it!

Can we... Fix it?

All About WENDY

Wendy is Bob's business partner in Bob's yard. She answers the phone and writes letters and uses the computer. Wendy also helps Bob with his building jobs when he is very busy. Wendy makes sure that Bob and Scoop and the others get to the right jobs at the right time.

Wendy's favourite thing is her garden with its pergola, patio and beautiful plants.

Look carefully!

How many differences can you find in these two pictures of Bob and his team?

Runaway Roley

Bob, Roley and Muck had been laying pipes into a trench all day, and they were tired. When Roley nearly rolled into a fence, and Muck's digger nearly knocked it down, Bob decided it was time for a rest.

"We'll finish the job tomorrow," he said.

Wendy was waiting to go home when they got back to the yard.

Bob yawned. "Sorry we're late," he said. "It's been a very long day."

Roley was already in the lean-to. "The longest day ever ..." he said, and fell asleep.

When Wendy went into the yard the next morning, Muck and Roley were still asleep. But Dizzy and the others were wide awake. "Hello, Wendy," said Dizzy. "What jobs have we got to do today?"

Wendy went into the office to check.

Dizzy and the others did not see Roley rolling towards the yard gates. He was still fast asleep! Pilchard tried to stop him, but she couldn't. "Miaow!" she said, and tried to tell the others about Roley. But no one was listening ...

At Farmer Pickles' farm, Spud the scarecrow was sleeping under an apple tree when Roley rumbled past. The ground trembled, the tree shook, and apples fell off and landed on Spud. "Ouch!" he said. "What's going on!"

Travis the tractor was in the field when he heard Roley coming. "Hello, Roley!" he said.

But Roley did not reply. He was still fast asleep, and Travis had to move out of the way as he went by. "I think Roley is sleep walking," said Travis. "Or sleep rolling!"

Back at the yard, Bob was

ready to start work. "Right, Muck, Roley," he said. "Can we fix it?"

"Yes we can!" said Muck.

Bob looked around. "Where's Roley?" he said.

Pilchard pointed to the gates, but Bob didn't notice.

Just then Bird landed on Scoop. "Bird says Roley is sleep walking!" said Scoop. "He's heading into town!"

"We have to find him," said Bob.

"Can we stop him?" said Scoop.

"Yes we can!" said the others.

"Er, yes, I think so ..." said Lofty.

"We've got to wake Roley up before he gets into trouble," said Bob.

"No," said Wendy. "It can be very confusing for someone if they get woken up miles away from where they've gone to sleep. We need to bring Roley back here before he wakes up."

"Right," said Bob. He turned to the machines. "Can we fix it?"

"Yes we can!" they said.

"Er, well, I think so ..." said Lofty.

Bob and Scoop looked for Roley. Dizzy and Muck looked for Roley. Wendy and Lofty looked for Roley, who was rumbling through the town, bumping into lamp posts and knocking over bins.

Suddenly, Scoop spotted Roley. "There he is!" he said.

"Oh, no!" said Bob. "He's near the big pipe trench we dug yesterday. If he falls in, we'll never get him out." Bob knew what to do. He took down the safety barrier and lay it across the trench, like a little bridge. It groaned as Roley rumbled over it. He rocked from side to side, but he made it across.

Bob rang Wendy on his mobile to let her know where Roley was.

Wendy brought Lofty, and Bob fixed Lofty's hook to Roley's front end. "Right," he said. "Take him back to the yard now, Lofty. But try not to wake him up."

Roley was soon back in his lean-to, still fast asleep.

"Hoo! I'm worn out," said Bob.

"Me too," said Lofty.

Later, when Muck and Dizzy got back, they rushed over to see Roley.

"Roley!" said Muck.

"Hurray!" said Dizzy.

Roley mumbled, shook – and woke up. "Oh, hi, everyone," he said. "Time to get up, eh? I've had a really good sleep. I can't wait to get back to the pipe laying job. Come on, Muck, let's ..."

But Muck was fast asleep. So was Dizzy. And Lofty. And Scoop.

Roley was puzzled. He turned to Bob. "Can we fix it?" he said.

Bob looked very sleepy. "I'm afraid not, Roley," he said. "We're all a bit tired. I think we'd better have the rest of the day off." He walked to his house. "See you tomorrow." Wendy waved to Bob as she set off for home.

"What's happening, Bird?" said Roley. "Look at them, all fast asleep. And I was the one who worked my rollers off yesterday. I can't understand it!"

21

All About SCOOP

Scoop is a digger, and the leader of the machines in Bob's yard. He's big and strong, but he's kind and gentle, too. He's always ready to help anyone in trouble – including Bob!

Scoop is good at solving problems, and he's full of bright ideas. He cheerleads the team before a job, "Can we fix it?"

Scoop rules OK!

All About LOFTY

Lofty's favourite saying is "er ... yeah I think so".

Lofty is a tall mobile crane. He worries about all sorts of things, and he talks to himself when he feels nervous. He feels better when Bob and the others tell him he's doing well.

Lofty is scared of just about everything – even heights, which is odd for a crane! He doesn't like stretching up too high in case he feels giddy!

Picture Puzzles

There is one piece missing in the picture of Travis and Spud. Which puzzle piece will finish the big picture?

Choose one of the little puzzle pieces to complete the big picture of Dizzy.

Bob's Big Surprise

Wendy was going to stay with her sister. "Mrs Potts will be here in the morning, Bob," she said. "She'll look after the office work while I'm away."

"Don't worry about us, Wendy," said Bob. "You just enjoy your visit."

"Oh, I will," said Wendy as she set off for the station with Scoop. "My sister's got a lovely garden, with a patio. If I had the time, I'd make my garden just like it ..."

"I miss Wendy when she's not here," said Dizzy.

"Not to worry, Dizzy," said Bob. "She'll be back tomorrow night. And we'll be too busy to miss her, because we're going to fix her garden as a surprise so it's as nice as her sister's."

Next morning, Mrs Potts rang. She told Bob she was ill, and couldn't help in the office.

Bob told the machines. "But

we'll manage," he said. "I'll put the telephone answering machine on, and pop back to check the messages. Now, let's go to work on Wendy's garden."

"Can we fix it?" said Scoop.

"Yes we can!" said Scoop, Muck, Dizzy and Roley.

"Er, yeah, I think so ..." said Lofty.

"Right then," said Bob. "Scoop, Roley, you two go to the garden centre and pick up the grass and tubs I ordered."

"No problem, Bob!" said Scoop.

"Muck, Dizzy, Lofty, you three come with me," said Bob. "You're on gardening duties."

There was a lot to do on Wendy's garden, so Bob made a list. "We'll put grass in the middle," he said. "And a patio by the house, with a pergola at the side."

"Er, what's a pergola, Bob?" asked Lofty.

Bob explained. "It's a place to sit in, made of wood."

"Can we have some flowers please, Bob?" Dizzy said. "Wendy loves flowers."

"Good idea, Dizzy," said Bob. "I'll order them later."

Muck used his scoop to make a flat place for the patio. Dizzy mixed mortar to stick the paving stones down. Lofty carried wood for the pergola. Bob used pegs and string to mark out where the flower bed would go.

Back in the office, Pilchard was trying to sleep when the phone rang, BRRRRRING! and she opened one eye. She opened her other eye when the fax machine went BRRRRRING, WHHHHHHIR! Then the message Wendy had recorded on the telephone answering machine started. "Please leave a message after the beep ..." BEEEEP!

Poor Pilchard couldn't sleep! She put her paws over her ears. "WAAAAOOOH!"

Bob and the others were working hard. Muck dug the soil for the flower beds and Dizzy poured mortar for the patio. Lofty

28

took wood to Bob, who nailed it together to make a pergola.

Bob looked at his watch. "I'm going to see if there are any messages at the office," he said. "I'll order the flowers, too."

Pilchard was still trying to get to sleep. When the phone rang again, BRRRRRING!, she knocked the receiver off the hook, then lay in the paper tray.

Just then Bob came in. "Goodness!" he said. "Now, how did that happen?" The red light was blinking on the answering machine. "Oh, no, there's lots of messages!"

Bob pressed a button. Gabble, gabble went the tape. He pressed another button, but still couldn't get the messages.

Instead, Bob sent a fax message to order the flowers, then saw the clock on the wall. "Three o'clock!" he said. "I'd better get back."

Bob got back to Wendy's garden just as Scoop and Roley arrived. "Great," said Bob. "Now we've got the stuff from the

garden centre, we can finish the job. Dizzy, you and Muck go and pick up the flowers I ordered."

"Oh, goodee!" said Dizzy.

Back in the office, Pilchard was sleeping until the phone rang again, BRRRIIING! Then the answering machine said, "Please lee-eeave a-a-a mesggegaftnfn ..."

"Waaarrrohh!" said Pilchard, holding her paws to her ears. That machine had to go ...

At Wendy's garden, Roley rolled the new grass flat and Scoop put plant tubs on the patio while Lofty and Bob built the pergola.

Bob's next job was to put the plants in the flower bed. "Oh, no! I've forgotten my fork," said Bob, jumping on to Lofty's step. "Come on," he said. "I need a lift back to the yard."

There were some surprises waiting for Bob. The receiver was off the phone, and a cushion was pushed into the top of the fax machine. The

answering machine was open, and Pilchard lay asleep amongst the mess.

"Oh my goodness! What's happened here?" said Bob. Pilchard opened one eye and looked at Bob. "It's no good looking innocent, Pilchard," said Bob. Then he saw the clock. "Six o'clock! Wendy will be back soon!" he said, and he grabbed his fork and rushed back to the garden.

Bob planted the flowers while Scoop went to get Wendy from the station. When she arrived home Bob took her into the garden. "Surprise, surprise, Wendy!" said Bob.

"Oh, Bob!" said Wendy. "It's lovely. There's a patio ... a place to sit ... and all my favourite flowers. Thank you, all of you!"

Later on, Bob and Wendy had a cup of tea on the new patio. "Did Mrs Potts manage in the office?" asked Wendy.

"Well," said Bob, "she phoned in sick, so things are in a mess. Could you come in early and sort it out?"

Wendy smiled. "Of course," she said. "Because then after work I can sit in my lovely garden and ... ooh, do you think I should have a fountain, Bob?"

Poor Bob! He didn't say anything, not a word!

All About MUCK

Muck is a digger dumper truck. He's very good at dumping and digging with his big scoop. He's often covered in muck and mud, but he's a very hard worker. He's ready for anything, and finds it very easy to get into trouble!

When Muck gets excited he gets his words mixed up. Muck is scared of just one thing – the dark!

Muck's best friend **Dizzy**

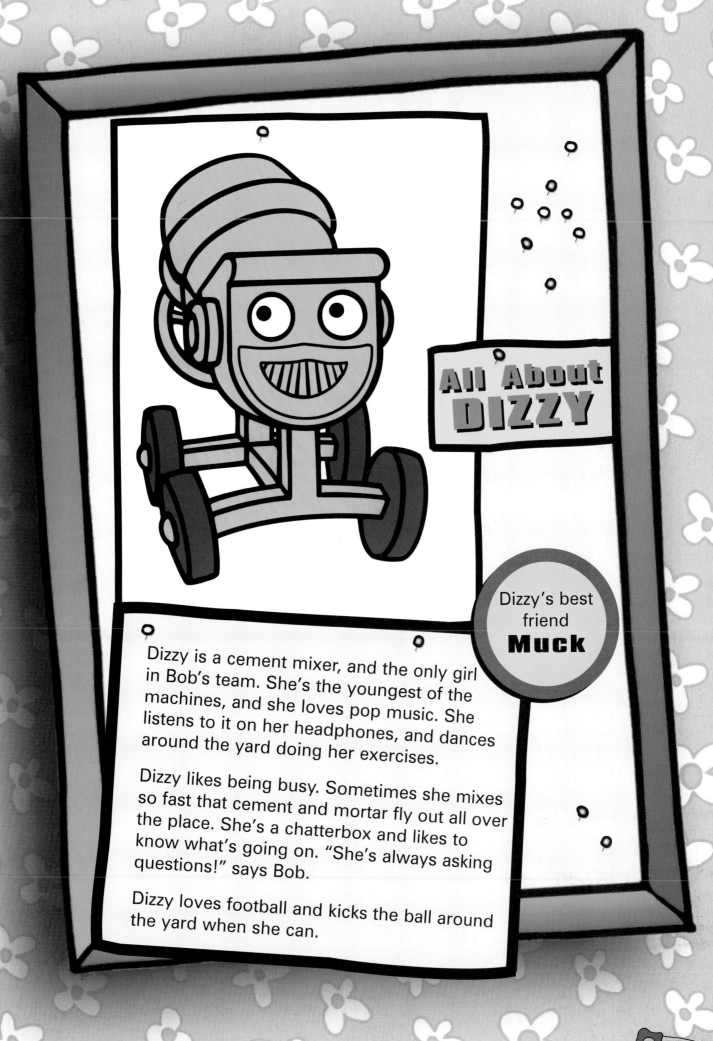

All About DIZZY

Dizzy's best friend **Muck**

Dizzy is a cement mixer, and the only girl in Bob's team. She's the youngest of the machines, and she loves pop music. She listens to it on her headphones, and dances around the yard doing her exercises.

Dizzy likes being busy. Sometimes she mixes so fast that cement and mortar fly out all over the place. She's a chatterbox and likes to know what's going on. "She's always asking questions!" says Bob.

Dizzy loves football and kicks the ball around the yard when she can.

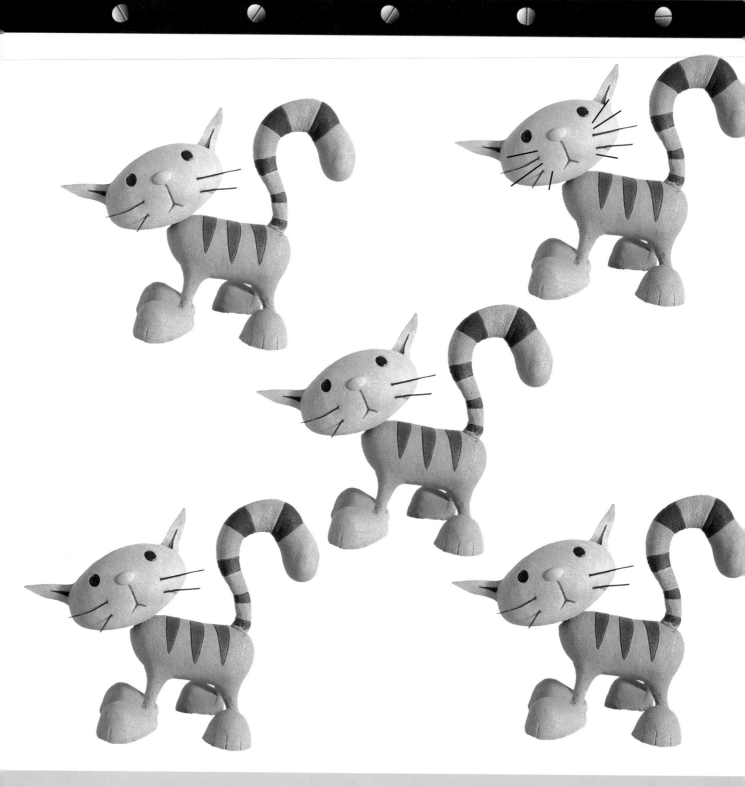

Look at the pictures of Bob's cat, Pilchard.
Which picture is different? Point to the odd one out.

Two the Same

Look at the pictures of Bird.

Can you find two that are the same?

Muck Gets Stuck

"What work are we doing today, Wendy?" Bob asked.

"There are some repairs to do in the tunnel," said Wendy. "You'll need to take the generator to work the lights, Bob. The main power is going to be switched off."

"Right," said Bob.

"Lofty has to go to Farmer Pickles' to move some tree trunks," said Wendy.

"We'd better get a move on then," said Bob.

Scoop, Muck and Lofty were soon ready. "OK, team, let's hit the road," said Bob.

"Can we fix it?" said Scoop.

"Yes we can!" said Muck.

"Um, yeah, I think so," said Lofty.

Bob, Scoop and Muck

stopped outside the entrance to the tunnel. "Muck, you take the bricks into the tunnel," said Bob.

Muck stopped at the entrance of the tunnel. "Uh-oh!" he said.

"What's up?" asked Bob.

"It's ... um ... all d ... dark and h ... horrible in here," said Muck.

Bob laughed. "We'll soon fix that!" he said. "I'll start the generator, then we can turn the lights on."

Bob pressed the starter button. The generator wobbled and clanked. Then it coughed and spluttered, and whizzed and whirred. "Er, it should be all right," he said.

Muck sounded worried. "What do you mean, 'should be'?"

Scoop made fun of him. "Muck's a scaredy truck!" he sang.

"I am not!" said Muck, and he closed his eyes and rushed into the tunnel.

It was very dark and dim inside. "Oo, er," said Muck. He

tried to tell himself not to be scared. "It's not really dark," he said as he tipped out his load of bricks. "Not really ..."

Back at the yard, Pilchard jumped into Dizzy's barrel.

Dizzy laughed. "Let's go for a ride," she said. "Well go and see Lofty at Farmer Pickles' farm."

"Miaow," said Pilchard.

"See you later," said Roley.

Bob went into the tunnel and left Scoop to look after the generator. It shook, it wheezed, and it groaned. Then it shivered and gasped, and went quiet. It had stopped working. "Uh-oh," said Scoop.

"Oh dear," said Bob as the lights went off. He walked back to the tunnel entrance to see what was wrong.

"Noooooo!" said Muck all alone inside the dark tunnel. "Turn the lights on! QUICK!"

Scoop peered into the tunnel. "Will Muck be all right?" he asked. "It's very dark in there."

"Scoop, are you telling me that Muck is afraid of the dark?" Bob asked.

Scoop nodded. "Yes."

"Oh, dear!" said Bob, and he quickly went back into the tunnel to get Muck.

Muck was very scared. "Not fun, not fun," he said.

"Come on," said Bob. "Follow me. Look, I've got a torch."

Muck was still scared. "No can do, Bob," he said. "I can't move. It's too dark."

"Oh ... right," said Bob, and he went outside again.

"Where's Muck?" asked Scoop.

"Stuck," said Bob. "Muck is stuck."

"I've got an idea," said Scoop, and he told Bob all about it.

At the farm, Dizzy and Pilchard were watching Lofty load logs on to Travis the tractor's trailer. They were surprised when Bob and Scoop arrived.

"Lofty, we need your help!" said Bob.

"Follow me to the tunnel!" said Scoop.

"What was all that about, Pilchard?" said Dizzy. "Pilchard?"

But Pilchard did not answer. She had gone for a ride in Scoop's digger!

Muck was still stuck in the tunnel when he heard the sound of an engine. "Who's that?" he whispered.

"It's me," said Lofty. "What's wrong, Muck?"

"I don't like the dark!" said Muck.

"Oh, I see," said Lofty. "It's a bit like me. I'm scared of heights. But don't worry, everyone's afraid of something. Just follow me. Stay close."

But Muck did not move. "It's too dark, Lofty," he said. "I can't do it. I can't."

Lofty came out of the tunnel on his own. "Muck's really, really stuck," he told Bob and Scoop.

They did not see Pilchard walking into the tunnel ...

Inside, Muck shook, and waited, and worried. Then, "Raaaoooww!" went Pilchard. "RAAAOOOWW!"

"Aaaarrgh!" said Muck. "A ... g ... ghost!" And he rushed out of the tunnel as fast as his tracks would carry him!

"Well, I'll be blowed," said Bob. "I thought you were stuck in there for good, Muck."

"Me too!" said Muck.

That night, back at the yard, Muck had a lot to tell Roley.

"After the wailing noise – whooo, whooo – I heard chains clanking – clank, clank – and shuffling footsteps – shuffle, shuffle. Then it went cold ... and I knew it was – a ghost!"

"I bet you were scared!" said Roley.

Muck looked pleased with himself. "Nah," he said. "But I got out of there – fast!"

"Cor!" said Roley. "You are brave, Muck!"

All About
Roley and Bird

Roley is a steam roller, and he's the most laid back of Bob's machines. He likes to doze and dream and think and take it easy. He likes to listen to music, and even makes up his own tunes.

Bird likes music, too, so she and Roley are good friends. Bird can only talk in whistles, but Roley and the other machines always know what she's saying.

What Can You Find?

Can you find all these things in the big picture?

Point to them and say the names.

Bob's Barn Raising

Bob was having his morning cup of tea with Pilchard and listening to the weather report on TV. "Oh dear, Pilchard," said Bob. "Bad weather is on the way."

Out in the yard, Dizzy was doing her exercises with her headphones on. "To the left, two, three," she said. "And stretch, two, three, and spin, two, three."

Bob and Wendy came out of the office.

"What are we doing today?" asked Scoop.

"Well, I need you and Lofty to help me mend Farmer Pickles' old barn," said Bob. "And Farmer Pickles needs Muck to help with the hay harvest."

"Can we fix it?" said Scoop.

"Yes we can!" said the others.

All except Lofty. "Er, yeah, I think so," he said.

The old barn was falling down. Bob nailed a piece of wood to one of the beams, but it fell off! "Oh, no," he said. "The beam is rotten. We'll have to get a new one. If Farmer Pickles puts any hay bales up there the floor will collapse."

At Farmer Pickles' field Muck collected the bales of hay, while Farmer Pickles stacked them one on top of the other.

Spud, who was hiding behind a bush, decided to have some fun. As soon as Farmer Pickles stacked a bale, Spud moved it away. "There's something funny going on here," said Farmer Pickles, and Spud burst out laughing. "It's you, Spud," said Farmer Pickles. "I might have guessed."

"I thought I'd help out with the harvest, Farmer Pickles," said Spud.

"Well maybe you can do something really useful like help me load the hay bales, instead

of unloading them," said Farmer Pickles.

Spud didn't like the sound of that. "Er, I have to get back to my proper job," he said. "You know, scaring birds, like this." Spud flapped his arms and hurried away.

Travis arrived at the field and Farmer Pickles and Muck loaded the bales of hay on to Travis's trailer. "Well done, you two," said Farmer Pickles as he looked at the dark sky. "I hope we can get the hay into the barn before the storm arrives."

Just then there was a flash of lightning, and the sky was darkening.

At the barn, Bob nailed the last bit of wood in place. "This new beam's as solid as a rock," said Bob. The thunder boomed. "Oh dear," he said, and started to count once he saw the next flash of lightning. "One elephant, two elephant, three elephant, four elephant, five elephant, six elephant, seven elephant, eight elephant." There was a rumble of thunder.

Scoop was puzzled. "Why are you counting elephants, Bob?" he asked.

Bob explained. "I'm counting the seconds between the lightning and thunder. It takes one second to say elephant, and I counted to eight before the thunder. That means the storm is eight miles away."

"Oh, I understand," said Scoop.

"Well, the barn is ready," Bob said. "But where is Farmer Pickles and the harvest?"

"He must be stuck behind the elephants ..." said Scoop.

Travis and Muck got to the barn. "We need to get the hay into the barn right away," said Bob.

"Can we load it?" said Scoop.

"Yes we can!" said the others.

"Er, yeah, I think so," said Lofty.

The job didn't take long with everyone helping. "This is the last bale, Bob," said Farmer Pickles. He looked around at the stacks of hay. "Now that's what I call a fine harvest."

"And that's what I call a fine barn!" said Bob. "Come on you lot, let's go home before we all get wet."

CRACK! went the lightning.

BA-DOOM! went the thunder as Bob and the machines travelled home.

As the rain started to fall the machines were under their lean-tos in the yard and Bob was in his house.

Spud ran for shelter amongst the hay in Farmer Pickles' barn and fell asleep.

All About SPUD

Spud is a cheeky scarecrow who lives on Farmer Pickles' farm. His job is to scare the birds away from the field, but he doesn't like real work much. Spud enjoys mischief, tricks and jokes!

Spud just likes to have a laugh and a giggle. If he does get too cheeky Farmer Pickles soon tells him to get, "Back to work!"

Spud's on the job, Bob!

All About TRAVIS

Travis is a tractor who lives and works on Farmer Pickles' farm. He's tough and strong and pulls his trailer along.

Travis is always ready to help Bob and his team, carrying heavy loads of pipes, bricks and wood. If Travis gets into trouble you can bet that Spud is not far away!

Bob's Hammer

Bob is always losing things. He puts his tools down, then forgets where they are.
Can you help Bob find his hammer and some nails?
Look hard – they are hidden in the yard!

It's time for a break, but before Bob can have a cup of tea, he has to find some saws that are hidden in the office. Can you help Bob find the saws?
How many can you find?

55

Buffalo Bob

Bob and his team were hard at work in Farmer Pickles' field.

Lofty used his scoop to lift bales of hay from Travis the tractor's trailer. He also lifted planks of wood and laid them flat on the ground.

Bob hammered nails into the planks of wood to hold them together.

Muck used his scoop to move the hay bales to the edge of the planks.

"A wooden floor, in a field?" said Muck. "What's going on, Scoop?"

"We're making a special flat place to dance," said Scoop. "It's for the line dancing contest tonight."

"Line dancing?" said Lofty. "What's that?"

Bob explained. "It's American dancing, like cowboys do. You wear cowboy clothes and dance in lines. Look, I'll show you." Bob showed the machines a few steps. "Take your partner by the hand, step to the left and swing 'em round. Take a step to the right and do a jump, and ..."

"You're pretty good, Bob!" said Muck.

"Thanks," said Bob. "I've entered tonight's contest with Mavis from the post office. We've been having lessons."

Things were nearly ready. Bob tapped the microphone. "One, two, testing, testing," he said, and his voice boomed out over the field. "Good, that's working," he said. "But it's getting late, and I have to get home for a bit of last-minute practice. Scoop, you're in charge."

"No problem, Bob," said Scoop. "Can we fix it?"

"Yes we can!" said Muck.

"Er, yeah, I think so," said Lofty.

When Bob had gone, Scoop, Muck and Lofty tried a few line dancing steps. "Forward, two, three, side, two, three, four ..."

Bob was practising at home. "I like the music," said Dizzy, and she danced around on two wheels so fast that Pilchard, who was sitting on her, had to hang on tight.

"Yee-hah!" said Dizzy.

"Raaaooowww!" said Pilchard.

Bob was daydreaming about winning the line dancing contest when Wendy came in. "Phone, Bob. It's Mavis," she said.

Bob talked to Mavis. "Oh, no!" he said. "On the jogging machine? Oh, well, never mind. Bye."

"Bad news?" asked Wendy.

Bob nodded. "Mavis has twisted her ankle. She can't dance tonight. I'll have to cancel our entry."

"Don't do that, Bob," said Wendy. "You could dance with

someone else – me!"

"You?" said Bob. "Can you line dance?"

"No, but I can learn!" said Wendy.

Bob and Wendy practised hard. Wendy was very good, and Bob was pleased. "Yee-hah! You learn fast, Wendy," said Bob. "Now, off you go, it's time to get ready for the contest!"

Wendy and Bob were wearing their cowboy outfits when Muck, Scoop and Lofty got back to the yard.

"Bye! Wish us luck," said Bob.

"Can they win it?" said Scoop. The machines cheered and whistled. "Yes they can!"

"Er, yes ... I think so," said Lofty.

"I wish we could be in the contest," said Dizzy.

"Yeah, line dancing is fun," said Scoop. "And Bob showed us a few steps. Hey, I've got an

idea! Pilchard, we need your help."

A few minutes later, Pilchard used her nose to push the button on Bob's stereo, and line dancing music filled the yard. Scoop, Muck and Lofty showed Roley and Dizzy what to do, then they all joined in. It was good fun!

When it got dark, Muck and Dizzy went into their lean-to, but they were too excited to sleep. "I can't wait to find out if Bob and Wendy won," said Dizzy.

After the contest, Bob took Wendy home. "Thanks for a lovely time, Bob," said Wendy.

"Thank you, ma'am," Bob said in his best cowboy voice. "You surely were a great partner."

"So were you, Bob," said

Wendy. "Night, Bob."

"Night, Wendy."

Bob was walking across the yard on tiptoes when Muck said, "Psst! Bob!"

"Did you win?" asked Dizzy.

Bob held up a big cup. "Well, yes ... yes, WE WON!" he said.

The machines were all wide awake now. They cheered and clapped and whistled. "Three cheers for Bob and Wendy!" said Scoop. "Hip, hip ..."

"Hooray!" said the others.

Wendy heard the machines cheering and shouting. She smiled a big smile and threw her cowboy hat high into the air. "Yee-hah!"